FORBIDDEN APPEAL

EVIE ROSE

Copyright © 2023 by Evie Rose

All rights reserved.

No part of this book may be reproduced in any form or by any electronic or mechanical means, including information storage and retrieval systems, without written permission from the author, except for the use of brief quotations in a book review.

This story is a work of fiction. Names, characters, places, and incidents are the product of the author's imagination or are used fictitiously. Any resemblance to actual events, locales, or persons, living or dead, is coincidental.

Cover: © 2023 by Cormar Covers.

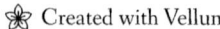 Created with Vellum

CONTENT NOTES

These content notes are made available so readers can inform themselves if they want to. They're based on movie classification notes. Some readers might consider these as 'spoilers'.

- Bad language: frequent
- Sex: fully described sex scenes with dirty talk
- Violence: on and off page
- Other: death of parent, death of side characters (including a family member), dubious consent, age gap, primal play, taboo relationship, praise kink

1

MIA

Look, usually, I love snow. What's not to like? It's beautiful. Stars falling from the sky, covering the ground like a soft blank sheet of paper. New. Untouched. Perfect.

But I'm making an exception.

Because this snow might stop me from getting to James McQuoid.

My knuckles are white on the steering wheel. The windscreen wipers are swooshing back and forth like an over-enthusiastic dog's tail, and the heaters are blasting. The car slides all over the place and I really hope I get to my dad's best friend's remote Scottish castle soon. Preferably before I lose control and end up in a ditch.

It began snowing about half an hour ago, almost the same time I turned off the main road, and now the road is only distinguishable from the fields by the little spikes of green sticking out, or the smoothness of the underlying tarmac.

All the way from London I've been rolling around in my head ideas of alternatives, and coming up with nothing.

My choices are these: accept the arranged marriage to a

man who looked at me like I was a slab of juicy meat, or find my way to the only person who might help me, and plead.

I thought about other options. Running away maybe. But my sheltered life means I haven't a hope of outrunning my uncle's mafia for more than a couple of days. I don't even have a passport.

I have no money, no friends, no family. My entire world is this beaten-up old land rover and a square of white linen. I clutch the napkin between my palm and the steering wheel like it's a comfort blanket. I know every word on it by heart, but brought it all the same. And I can't stop touching it, like if I let it go it might disappear, or he won't be there when I arrive.

I can't let myself think about that. He'll be there. He has to be, because if I get to the end of this... well I'm calling it a road but who knows really... If I get to the end of this journey and he's not there, I suspect that will break me in a way my uncle hasn't managed in three long solitary years.

I still remember when James gave me the napkin. My treasure map. We were in the Indian restaurant we went to every month, the three of us. My dad, James, and me.

In my memory those evenings are a kaleidoscope of colour and taste, almost too much for my senses to take in. The smell of incense and cumin, the yellow light refracted through brass fittings with blurred geometric patterns. The crack of poppadoms and the sour tang of lime pickle with a kick of chilli. My fingers covered with buttery ghee and the sweet scent of garlic on pillowy naan bread.

I loved every moment of those dinners with them. Both of them.

We had rambling conversations. Sometimes James and my dad would talk shop, occasionally getting heated about some moral or financial controversy as they drank pints of bubbly lager that coated their stubbly top lips in white foam. But usually it was all fun and banter. My dad teased James about being a ladies' man, and James always denied it with a grumpy growl.

It wasn't until I was in my teens that I began to be weirdly jealous of James' hypothetical women. The ones he maintained didn't even exist. My heart started to flutter when he pulled me in for a hug when we arrived. A silly crush.

When I think about it now, it was weird to go for a curry every month with two dangerous, powerful mafia bosses. Dad told me once that I was the perfect excuse. He took his daughter for dinner, and no one suspected he was catching up with his old friend. Because kingpins ought not to be friends. Not part of the code of toxic masculinity, or something. All I know is that all my life there was me and my dad and James. I didn't see Dad that much day to day, he was always busy. But once a month, like clockwork, we would go out.

One night, there was news about a nuclear threat. James' green eyes—more compelling and inspiring than any nature program about the jungle—went serious. Grabbing up the fourth napkin on the table, he unfolded it and dug a pen from the pocket of the suit jacket he'd discarded hours earlier.

"You drive to Inverness, then you take the road north. After an hour, you turn off to the right towards the mountain that looks like this." He drew an outline on the fabric. Then like an illustrated map at the front of a fantasy novel, he talked me through the route to his remote Scottish castle.

He gave me the napkin with a smile, and said, "There are three people in the world who know where my home is."

And now, I guess there are two.

It was thick cotton, none of that flimsy disposable stuff. Heavy like a promise.

I protested this was stealing, and James smirked and said that it was high time I began my life of crime, given my family. My dad rolled his eyes, and I saw him leave a hefty tip to make up for James' and my theft.

I hid the map in my underwear drawer and took it out from time to time. I imagined myself finding a way to go north and find him.

But I didn't, because he hadn't come for me after Dad died. Not even a condolence card with a picture of a lily and some trite phrase.

After my father's death, I was unfulfilled and unloved. Lonely. But no one bothered with me much, and I managed.

But being trapped for the rest of my life, in marriage?

No. No way.

I round a corner and the castle looms suddenly out of the flickering white. Shit. This is it.

I'm trembling as I slide the car to a halt randomly on a flat patch that I hope is solid underneath the snow. I tuck the napkin into the glove compartment and smooth my messy hair. I'm all set.

Except for. You know. Any idea of how I'm going to work up the nerve to ask James to help me.

He might have disappeared after my father was killed, but the thing is, I've had this bone-deep knowledge since I left London that if I can just get up here, to *him*, it will be okay. That I'll be able to do this. Somehow. Everything will be alright when I see James.

Rough grey stone, the castle towers above me, bleak and imposing. The walls look like they've been standing for a thousand years, and will for a thousand more.

I shiver. Snow settles on my forearm. A chill goes down my neck even though my blonde hair covers it, spilling over my shoulders.

The snow crunches beneath my feet as I approach the big wooden door. It hurts my knuckles when I knock, but hardly makes any noise. A mouse knock.

The door flies open.

"Get in," James growls and drags me into the porch, slamming the massive door behind us, his brows hard together.

He recognises me and I'm so relieved I could sob, though my stomach turns over as I look up into his face. He's as severe and unyielding as his castle. His shoulders are broader than I remember and the strong line of his jaw is covered in black stubble that blends to silver at his temples. Those green eyes, they're the same and have tiny lines at the corners, like they still crinkle when he laughs. His mouth, oh god his mouth is wide and his bottom lip is plush. I want to take it between my teeth and bite it. I want to suck...

I shouldn't feel this. He must be in his late thirties compared to my eighteen.

Experienced then, a voice at the back of my head whispers. *He'd make it good. He'd know exactly what to do to drive you out of your mind.*

No. It's bad enough that I've turned up out of nowhere, and I have to ask for his help because I have literally no one else. Do I really have to also be immediately attracted to my dad's best friend?

He seems to realise at the same time as I do that his hand is still gripping my upper arm and removes it slowly.

"You're freezing," he mutters, then strides away so fast I have to hustle to stay with him as the wood panel entrance porch of his castle opens into a vast feasting hall.

He practically shoves me in front of a crackling open fire, red and yellow flames jumping, then steps back. Like he doesn't trust himself.

"Is anyone following you? What happened?"

I'm in shock. Maybe that's why I simply stare at him. James is dressed in a pair of dark jeans that hug his thighs just the right amount to show there are muscles beneath, and a soft plaid blue and green cotton shirt, open at the neckline and revealing the dip of his clavicle and a few dark hairs. On top he has on a rustic woollen jumper in a dark green that matches his eyes and makes me want to dive right into him.

He looks good enough to eat with a spoon in greedy overflowing mouthfuls.

It's not as though I didn't know what he looked like, but I haven't seen him for three years. I used to get little tummy flutters when he'd do something kind for me and give me that big smile and twinkling eyes, I thought... Well, I thought that was just a childish fancy. A crush.

But no.

This is a full tug from deep in my stomach and below, heat swirling between my legs. This is not childish. This is weakened knees, hot blood pounding, and wetness flooding my core.

James. My dad's best friend. Is the most gorgeous man I've ever seen.

Even if he's scowling down at me.

"Are you being followed," he demands again, since I've been gaping at him rather than answering.

"I don't think so." If I had, they probably would have caught me by now. My teeth begin to chatter and I look to the fire, holding out my hands, but immediately my eyes slip back to James like he's a magnet and I'm base metal.

I should go. But the thought of accepting my lot in life and marrying my uncle's goon weighs me down with lead.

"Mia. My god you're..." James scans my face as though he can't believe it. His brows darken into a scowl. No hint of a smile. That shouldn't make him even more handsome, but his commanding tone makes me want to throw myself on his mercy. Amongst other things.

I swallow.

"Mia," he repeats in disbelief. And despite everything, my name in his voice is so sexy my insides go all shimmery and light.

Strong fingers grip my chin and force me to look into his eyes. I quake, and yet... I've never felt safer.

Until he growls, "Tell me why you're here."

I take a deep breath and state the simple truth. "To beg for your help."

2

JAMES

I gave instructions to a cute kid on how to find me if the worst happened. A forbidden woman has arrived.

Mia takes my breath away. I knew she was missing from Barnes, but didn't dare hope she'd come to me, my courageous lass. I'm going to murder my informant. He told me she was shy and reserved, but fundamentally safe and happy under her uncle's care. How could he not have found out about something so important that she fled all the way to Scotland?

She licks her lips and her eyes go wide, the pupils blown. Her hair is damp since the snow on it has begun to melt, and she's shaking from the cold.

I want to pull her into my arms and heat her with my body. I release her chin. Mia needs to warm up before we have this conversation.

"I'll always help you. But a hot drink first."

She nods gratefully.

I take her to the kitchen and while I make tea—with an obscene amount of sugar for her—I watch as she examines everything silently. I remember with a pang that she only ever knew me as a person in one space—the restaurant where we used to meet. She never saw my house in Chiswick. She takes in the abstract paintings on the wall. The plethora of ingredients in jars on shelves and the plush but unashamedly stark furnishings. It's simple, my home.

I can't believe she's here.

It brings back memories of the night Duncan died, not that they're ever far from my mind. Perhaps I should have gone on running the Chiswick mafia, but I'd been planning to get out for a long time, and Duncan's death felt like a fucking massive celestial hint. A message that, yeah, you've pushed your luck as far as it will go. No more.

Mia was tucked away in the Barnes' compound with her grief. I staked it out for a few days and she was with her uncle when I glimpsed her. Pink eyed and sad and so heartbreakingly young, she'd given him a wan smile. Any thoughts of taking her from her home died then. She needed her family, not to be taken to a lonely old Scottish castle.

Even so, I waited at the restaurant evening after evening for a week, thinking maybe she'd arrive and choose me. The grief gnawed away at my insides and told me she wasn't coming, and was better off without me.

I gently touch my palm to the small of her back to guide Mia to a big squashy chair in the living area and she slips her boots off and nestles in with a cautious glance at me, like a stray kitten waiting to be shouted at for curling into a blanket. Just like she used to when she was a kid, removing her shoes and sitting cross-legged on the benches of the Indian restaurant.

But there's no need for her fear. As long as she's in my home, she's welcome, and no one will tell her off for making herself comfortable.

She's wearing leggings and a grey sweatshirt. Her honey-blonde hair is loose around her shoulders, and those big blue eyes blink up at me.

"What happened," I prompt, and the weather obliges the moment with an ominous rumble of thunder.

"I don't want to get married," she whispers miserably, eyelashes fanning her cheeks as she looks at the floor. "I want freedom and to go to university, not to be gifted to a grunting mafioso."

Ah fuck. That sort of bullshit should have gone out of fashion along with powdered wigs and arsenic wallpaper.

"Your uncle is forcing you to marry?" He's dead. No one forces my lass to do anything she doesn't want to. I'll rain death and destitution on his pathetic life and crush his bones under my heel.

She drags her white teeth over her plump bottom lip and looks so sad my heart breaks as she nods.

I should have killed that bastard years ago. Duncan was too indulgent of his younger brother.

"Does he want you to marry someone in particular?" Because, you know, if he wanted her to marry me, he's still dead but I'll compromise on the bone crushing.

"One of his henchmen." She wraps her hands around her mug of tea like without it she might blow away. "I think he's my second cousin."

Back to his bones being powder then.

I nearly decree that I'll murder her fuckwit uncle and keep her safe here with me. But I hesitate, because she's eighteen and probably had enough of older men making decisions for her.

"And what did you hope I would do?" That leaves her the choice. Nominally. I'm still going to murder Logan Anderson.

"I thought..." Her gaze slides from mine and she fidgets. "I don't know. I thought you might be able to talk with my uncle?"

"Not talk, no." I moderate my tone, but still. My lip curls in disgust at the idea.

"Oh." She disguises her disappointed reaction by taking a sip of tea, then flits her blue eyes to me.

"But I can give you a new life and identity far from here. I won't let anyone hurt you," I admit gruffly.

Her shoulders lower, and that line between her brows smooths. That simple promise relaxing her fills me with absolute determination to do whatever is required. She is my sweet bonnie lass, and I'll provide *everything* she needs.

"The only reason you will get married is because you're desperately in love."

She nods but saying that seems to undo all the progress we've just made and she's tense again.

"Thank you, that's kind," she stammers out as she stands, tugging at the hem of her jumper. "I guess I should go—"

"You're not leaving," I interrupt.

Her gaze darts to mine, but instead of the shock I expect from my instinctive order, there's a mess of emotions. Everything from relief to fear to apprehension and hope.

Outside, the grey sky lights up cloud to cloud, then it's only a few seconds before the rumble arrives. The storm is drawing closer.

"It's thundersnow, mo chridhe." The endearment slips out without my permission. My heart. She has my heart in her delicate hands and doesn't even realise. "It's dangerous. Stay here until it clears." She came to me for help, and I'll protect her from her own bad impulses, as well as anyone else's.

Particularly mine.

"Mo-hrey-ya," she repeats the unknown Gaelic word softly and with an atrocious accent, then shakes herself. "I couldn't intrude."

"You wouldn't be." Or if she was, I'd want her to. She has no idea how much I adore her. But a wee bonnie lass doesn't need a jaded, scarred, grumpy retired mafia boss, however rich I am. Moreover, Duncan would murder me from the grave for how I feel about Mia.

She's here until the storm passes; that will have to be enough.

"Besides, it's getting dark." I nod to the window where the snow is almost half a foot thick. "How did you get the car?"

"Stole the Land Rover Dad used to let me use around the estate."

I can't help but laugh. "Your dad would have been proud."

"Dad always said I would need to be able to drive one day. The roads weren't as difficult as I thought they might be."

My face drops. "What? You'd never driven on a road before?"

"Yeah." She scrunches her nose. "The first big roundabout was a bit hairy."

My heart attempts to throw itself out of my mouth and gets stuck just below my Adam's apple. She drove from outside London to here, having never before driven on a public highway.

"Well, and all the multi-lane roads were... Yeah. It was okay."

It's a twelve-hour drive, minimum, and the last part was

in the damn snow. She's even braver and stronger than I realised.

"Did you bring anything with you?"

She looks at me like I'm an idiot. "Of course I did."

My heart slips down to where it should be, then sinks lower. It's a good thing she's got her own clothes. Absolutely. I wouldn't survive seeing her dressed in my shirt, covered with my scent, how dainty and small she is emphasised by the baggy fabric over her pert breasts... I grit my teeth. I'm pleased. I am.

"Let's get your stuff then."

I tug on boots in the porch and when I open the front door, it's clear the snow has been falling harder. There's another rumble of thunder.

I look across at the Land Rover with faded green paint. It's probably bugged to high heaven. We need to dispose of it, but she's not going anywhere. If anyone is getting struck by lightning, it's me.

"Give me the key."

She puts her car key into my palm and her fingertips skim my thumbpad.

It's the smallest touch, but electric. I jerk back like she burned me.

Our eyes meet and the hurt is naked and clear. Misery that I rejected her so viscerally.

Fuck.

I almost go to grasp her shoulder and reassure her. But I can't. If I feel her warmth again, my body will react and then we'll be in all sorts of trouble. We're stuck here, snowed in. I can't do anything that will make her scared of me. That means no touching.

When she was a kid, she'd sit on my knee and give me a

cuddle, all powdery wee bairn smell. I never shied away from her. And suddenly I wonder if I was right about leaving her with her uncle. Maybe she's been as starved of affection for these three years as I have. As lonely. It didn't occur to me to ask my spy in the Barnes mafia if she got hugs. My heartstrings constrict, but there's nothing to do now except keep her safe.

"Did you disable any trackers?"

"I couldn't find any. I'm not sure anyone else even remembered this vehicle existed. It was only used on the estate, and has barely been out of the barn since..." She tails off, but I understand. Duncan taught her to drive in that Land Rover, and no one has bothered with it—or I am beginning to suspect her—since he died.

"Fine. The risk is too high that there's some way of tracing it. I'll get your stuff then dispose—"

"No!" She's instantly distressed.

I shake my head. "What? Why?"

"I like it," she whispers.

"You like it?" It's a Land Rover, not a Highland Terrier puppy.

"It's... my friend. My only one," she mutters.

I heave in a breath and drag my fingers through my hair. Her *friend*? How alone has she been that a beaten-up vehicle is her only friend? I stare at her as she wrings her hands, but still, she's determined and grim.

"Okay." I glare up at the darkening clouds and lightning cracks across the sky. That'll block everything, including communication with my spy and any trackers, until the storm clears. After that I'll have to figure out another solution.

"You won't hurt it?" she asks, unsure.

"Promise." I'd never harm anything she cared about, even if it is just a car. "Stay here."

I run over and run my hand under the wheel arches and in other obvious places. Nothing. Yanking open the back door, I expect to haul out several suitcases.

But no. There's one small black rucksack. I throw it over my shoulder, and check, and check again. Not even a coat. Damn.

I'll buy one for her. More than one. She knows she can come here now. Maybe she'll visit and allow me to take care of her.

Maybe I won't let her leave.

I shove the thought away.

A sandwich wrapper is on the front passenger seat, and an empty bottle of fruit juice. Is that all she's eaten in a whole day? My lass must be starving. I'll fix that.

I return to the house, shaking off the snow as I enter. Mia presses her lips together as I give her the bag, as though she expects to be told off.

"Is that all of it?" I ask, although god knows where it would be. I just can't believe everything she cares about fits into that small rucksack.

"Yeah. Thanks." She fingers the canvas of the bag nervously and the sight of her hand clenching makes my cock rise with the fiction she would be tentative when she first touched my cock. Until I encouraged her. Showed her she couldn't hurt me, and I'd take anything she gave me.

I can't look at her.

"I'll provide everything else you need." I lose the promise into the door as I close it. Loud enough for her to hear, but I can't look at her while I say that in case my eyes indicate, *including orgasms and losing your virginity.* Because, yeah, my spy was enough of an arsehole to unsolicitedly tell me that she hadn't been with a man. It didn't bother me either way at the time. Now...

"Come." I push the thought away and lead her to the wooden staircase wide enough for five people to walk abreast. "We'll find you somewhere to sleep. And that was a long drive. You'll want to have a shower, right? Or there's a decent bath."

"Oh, yeah. That would be amazing if you don't mind. Are you sure? Is it only you here?" she doesn't give me time to reply as she trips after me, assuming I guess from my unbroken stride what my answer is. I'm very sure.

"Aye." Taking a left into the guest wing I open the first door into a guest bedroom I prepared back in the days after Duncan's death when I was thinking about a wee lass living here.

While she peers around as though she's never seen anything like it, I lean my hip against a chest of drawers. Convenient height, I notice. If I put Mia on it I could... Get my mind out of the gutter and not lust after a lass half my age. You'd think at thirty-seven I'd be able to control myself, and usually, yes. But Mia is temptation on a different level.

"I like..." She gestures at the cosy decor, all cream woollen tartan and solid pale oak. Her gaze skitters between me and the whimsical four-poster with floaty sheer curtains that dominates the room. "All of it."

I nod. It suits her, as I intended. "I'll make you dinner."

"You don't need to—"

She cuts off at my raised eyebrow.

"'Kay. Thank you." Lowering herself onto the bed, she stares out of the window, where the day is turning towards evening. White into grey into black and silver. With her hair falling over her shoulders, a bit messy now the snow has dissolved, she looks young and tired.

"How long do you think the storm will continue?" she asks.

I shrug when she peeks at me from the corner of her eye. If I had my way it would never stop, so she'd never leave. But that's why selfish kingpins don't get to control the weather. "It might ease tomorrow."

That doesn't seem to please her.

"When the weather has moved off I'll take you wherever you want to go in the helicopter. I'll sort you out a new life. Whatever you need."

Until then I'll spoil her and pretend she's here because she couldn't stay away. Because she came here, to me, to feel safe.

"James." Her back straightens as she rises, bracing herself. "The car. Is it going to be a problem?"

I don't know, but I shake my head. "No one can hurt you while you're here." Because they'd have to go through me, and I'd die before she so much as broke a fingernail or spent an hour with anyone she didn't like. Never mind *marry*.

"Why not forget about your uncle until the storm clears," I suggest, though it comes out as a decree.

She brightens. "So, we're just snowed in? No mafia stuff. We're... Us? Right?"

"Us," I repeat. Mia makes me want to deny reality. I want *us* to be *always*. "Aye."

She smiles shyly and damn, how am I supposed to keep my hands off her?

"Thank you," she whispers.

One evening of *us* will have to be enough to provide memories for a lifetime. Because though she wants freedom, I want *her*. On her knees. On her back. On my lap with my thick cock spearing her tight hot body. I'm already half erect and I need to get out of her room before I begin imagining her in the shower. Naked. Water streaming over her curves.

Fuck. This is going to be torture.

I turn away before I do something to scare her. The things I want, they're perverted. They'd terrify a sweet lass like her. I'll protect her until the storm passes, then send her to start a new life.

Untouched.

3

MIA

My tummy is rumbling by the time I find my way down to the kitchen. James looks up as I enter and all the pep talk I gave myself while I showered, about things being exactly as they were when I was a kid, hisses and melts and steams like a snowball tossed into an open fire.

From behind the kitchen island where he was chopping vegetables, he stills. His gaze drags down my body like he's in a trance, and I go flushed and hot as I was in the bath, but with the addition of a stronger throb between my legs. I shift, rubbing my thighs together subtly.

"Mia." He's around the work surface and by my side in an instant, then looks away, a flash of guilt in his eyes. Then his gaze returns to my face as though drawn there by a string, and mutters, "You look lovely."

I do?

He guides me to a stool at the kitchen island. In a semi-circle are pretty ceramic bowls in speckled blue-green and white all filled with nibbles that make my mouth water. His palm brushes on the small of my back as he skirts behind me.

"Food won't be long."

"You cooked for me?" How long has it been since anyone bothered to do anything for me alone?

"There's not much pizza delivery around here."

"Practically in the dark ages." I widen my eyes in mock horror.

"You'll get used to it."

As though I'll be coming for dinner with him again. That's even more mouth-watering than the smell from a pan on the massive navy range cooker labelled AGA.

The comment hangs in the air, not taken back or acknowledged. I watch as he ladles out the soup into sage green speckled bowls and rips off leafy green herbs to strew on the surface.

Then I see the table. Dark, aged wood, a bit beaten up. One end is set with two places, and a single candle. He lowers the lights, and indicates to me that I should sit. The whole thing is... Romantic. It gives the illusion I've been invited for dinner, rather than begged for help.

It's like a date.

He puts soup before me, more of a broth really, with generous shreds of white meat, chunks of carrot and circular slices of green. "What is it?"

"Cock-a-leekie."

I snort.

"It is not funny," he says, but he's smiling as he sits down.

"Chicken and leek. Why not call it that? Rather than..." Look I've never thought of myself as smutty, but leaking cock makes my brain jump to a vision of James holding his cock, pre-come beading at the tip.

Totally inappropriate.

He shrugs. "Words matter. Sometimes calling something innocent by a rude or fancy name enhances our enjoyment of it."

My insides go liquid. "Like a taboo?"

Our gazes meet and I wonder if he's thinking the same thing as I am. The taboo of my being his best friend's daughter. The taboo of him being almost twenty years older than me.

Would those taboos make it even better if we kissed? If we *more than kissed*?

"Eat your dinner," he grumbles. Then he leans back in his chair, arms crossed and waits implacably.

I tip soup onto my spoon and bring it to my mouth. He watches me as I taste it. Is he anxious about whether I like his food? The kingpin of Chiswick, as was? A man who left his power and brutality behind, and now is caring for a woman young enough to be his daughter?

The soup is a rich broth, salty and savoury and a whimper of enjoyment escapes me. I'm starving for this. Worth the wait of being hungry for half the day.

I devour the whole bowl so ravenously, my hair begins to slip from its ponytail. Opposite me, James eats at a steady pace, but when a strand falls forwards and touches my lip, and I sweep it back behind her ear, his movements stutter and he swallows before he takes the next mouthful. Like his throat is dry.

"Mmmm, that was delicious." I look right at him. "You'll have to give me the recipe so I can try to make it."

"It's a secret," he teases. "I could tell you, but I'd have to kill you."

"Tempting." Would the killing be in a sexy way? That would seal the deal. "But no. It wouldn't do any good anyway. I can't cook. When I've tried I burn everything and get chased out of the kitchens. Though I'll have to try, because I cannot live without this now. Regularly."

"Stay here and I'll make it for you wherever you want."

There's shock on his face despite the calm demeanour he delivered that invitation with. As though he can't believe he issued it. "Anyway, at least if you don't like the main course, you've eaten something."

"Wait what? Is there more?" My mouth drops open.

"That was the starter." He rolls his eyes as he gets to his feet.

"I am in so much trouble," I laugh, patting my stomach.

Next he brings me a tiny sorbet that he calls a palate cleanser. Like I'm in a fancy restaurant. I can't believe he's going to all this hassle *for me*.

Then roast grouse with wild mushrooms, watercress and crispy roast potatoes. It's the best thing I've eaten in a long, long time.

And between the food, he asks me how things have been. Tentatively at first, we share details of the last three years. I want to know about his disappearance. How he quit being a mafia boss when mostly death is the way people leave the mafia.

He's equally eager, or seems so, to hear about what happened to me. School, books, films. All the pets I wish I had. I guess he remembers from before, because when I boast that my grades are good he nods impatiently and says he knows that. But when I confess I don't have any friends, he listens in attentive silence, brows pinched together.

I quiz him about how he left everything behind, and it's not purely because I could do with the tips. I want to follow right in his footsteps all the way to his side.

The price has been every personal connection. I'm the only one who knew where he was, and I see a flare of sadness in his eyes when I ask him how he coped with the isolation. His answer, *fine*, is a lie.

He's been lonely.

"Dessert?" He changes the subject.

"Is it kulfi?" I ask.

"No, sorry," he laughs softly. I know he's remembering red velvet cushions, the steam of fragrant hot towels and the chill of sweet milky kulfi.

Those evenings were innocent when I was little. Colouring in pictures of flowers as I sat in our usual booth. I ate rice and chicken korma, and poppadoms. *So many* poppadoms with mango chutney. James would pile them onto my plate and challenge me to eat more than him.

When I was older, the colouring books were replaced by novels, the plain rice became pilau rice and sometimes James brought me the latest fantasy paperback with talking animals and world-ending stakes. In the years leading up to Dad's death, I listened. I chatted with them. They cast wary glances at each other when they discussed my uncle, disagreeing about him. Dad thought Uncle Logan was merely a pain. James maintained he was a problem in the waiting, though they didn't share the details. But when James teased my dad, his humour always bone dry, he would wink at me.

I was in on the joke, part of their team.

And this evening, it feels like James and I are a team again, just the two of us. "You didn't have to go to so much trouble."

"It's not." His green eyes pin me as he gathers up our empty plates.

"Can I help?" I need to be closer to him. I'm already slipping out of my chair and following him to the counter.

"No," he growls from behind the kitchen island,

partially blocked from view. He swallows and his throat bobs, his Adam's apple covered in black stubble. I want to kiss him there and feel that roughness on my lips.

"Stay there." He sounds hoarse, like he's enduring a trial. James braces himself, one hand on the work surface, eyes closed. It's as though he's in pain. "I only need to grab dessert."

I ignore him, of course, and round the kitchen island just in time to see him kneeling down to the under-counter. The fridge door is open and spilling golden light right onto his crotch. He rubs his palm over the long bulge in his jeans and mouths, *Fuck, Mia.*

Oh. Em. Gee.

He's hard.

And *massive*.

I take the two silent steps backwards so I can only see the top of his head.

"Shall we eat dessert in the sitting room?" I say guilelessly. There's only one way I'm going to get him close to me, and across a table isn't it.

That shiver of arousal I feel? It's mutual.

He wants me too.

4

JAMES

I look up and jolt to find Mia watching me from the other side of the worksurface, thank god for small mercies. Fresh-faced from her shower, rosy and sweet, her hair in a ponytail, she's a dream. I imagine all that silk released and wrapped over my fist. Just right for tugging—gently but firm enough to make her gasp.

That slouchy sweater and figure-hugging leggings. Her feet are clad just in socks. They're red with white snowflakes and altogether she looks so cute I want to... I don't know. I have no place in my life for cuteness like her.

Which is why I adjust my painfully erect cock, subtly, as I pull the cranachan from the fridge.

"Sure, that's a good idea." Perhaps in the lounge I'll stop imagining clearing the table with one sweep of my arm, then setting her on it and dining on her pussy, her thighs over my shoulders, until she screams, then screams again as I make her come time after time on my tongue until she's as melted as butter on a summer's day.

I direct her through to the smallest of the sitting rooms

and busy myself lighting a fire, even though it's easily warm enough. In alternating moans of pleasure and contented chatter, she identifies the ingredients of the Scottish dessert I made for her. Cream, raspberries, oats, whisky, honey.

And when I join her on the sofa—she has taken up camp right in the middle because she clearly has no idea how tempting her proximity is—I can't help but look at her.

"What is it?" she asks when she notices. "Have I got cream around my mouth? On my nose?" She touches the corresponding parts of her face as if I might be in doubt about what she means.

"Yes." I dip my finger into the cream of my dessert and dab it onto her nose and she squirms away, laughing.

That breaks a bit of the tension that has been building between us. Or my fantasies, anyway. My erection doesn't go down, but I can think clearly enough to keep her at a distance. We talk all evening. Recalling good times, but about plans for the future, too. Opinions of the antiques in the room and what she'd want in a house. What she likes—kids and animals. She's been thinking about studying to be a veterinarian but isn't sure about the commitment. And if she notices my jaw tightening when she says she'd love to have babies, she doesn't let on. With the right person, she adds, glancing at me under lowered lashes.

When the fire has died to red embers, she yawns and I realise I'm an arsehole. It's been an insane day of escape for her, and she's been awake forever.

"You should go to bed, mo chridhe." I stand and gather our bowls.

"I'll do that." She's at my side instantly, trying to lift them from my hands.

Her fingers are a hot vice as they touch mine: I can't ignore it, I can't think about anything else.

"No," I grunt. I take care of *her*. That's how this works.

"Let me do something! I haven't lifted a finger all evening."

"It was my pleasure." I jerk the bowls from her as she tries to wrest them from me. And I don't know how it happens but the next moment the empty china is bouncing off the carpet and Mia has her hands on my shoulders and is kissing me.

It's so unexpected it should make me freeze. But my body knows exactly what to do with this situation even as my mind protests.

I take control and for a glorious few seconds we're standing in front of the heat of the fire, our mouths giving and taking in a slide against each other. Her kiss is all inexperienced ardour. Her sweet curves are pressed to my front, my head is bowed to reach her and she's on tiptoes.

Her whimper of need has my grip tightening on her waist and finally wakes me to what I'm about. I absolutely cannot do anything more than kiss her, and if we don't stop now I'll have her naked and be making her come with my mouth within three minutes.

It takes all my strength to peel her arms from around my neck, but before I can step away, she grabs me, tiny and furious.

"Don't you dare deny me, James. Don't you dare."

You don't take advantage of a lass tipsy on whisky-laced desserts, who are snowed in.

She said she wants freedom. She's your best friend's daughter.

The lucid and logical part of my mind is an uptight prick, and I hate him.

"I shouldn't," I protest but Mia must know. She must

hear how weak I am for her, because she says that one word designed to undo me.

"Please."

With a groan, I tug Mia back into my arms and fall onto the sofa. She scrambles to sit across my lap and get our lips together again.

"Just a kiss," I tell her.

She makes a sound that could mean anything from *yes* to *no* to *that feels good* to *shut up and kiss me*. Functionally, it means that last one, as her mouth lands on mine with infectious enthusiasm.

I'm so fucking happy she's here. Not just in my castle, where I can protect her, but seated across my thighs. She's delicious. So sweet she'll give me diabetes and I don't care, I want all of it.

I should not be doing this with my best friend's daughter.

But I'm only stealing a wee taste, so much less than I want, it seems as though my restraint in not doing more should be sufficient to absolve me of the crime. I'm not doing anything irrevocable. I'm not taking everything this innocent lass doesn't even realise she's offering.

But this kiss is so amazing it's ripping me apart. I'm torn into shreds for Mia, all my certainty in smithereens. I imagined I knew Mia and myself, and the relationship we had. But no. This lass whose heart I know so well but whose body has turned into a woman's while I wasn't watching is everything to me. Our kiss is a mix of all of these conflicted emotions. The desire and the taboo and the deep knowledge that she's both the cute lassie I cared for and this woman I admire and want and adore. Need. Love.

Fuck, I *love* Mia.

The combination of our longstanding friendship and

combustible attraction is heady and undeniable. My feelings for Mia are in my bones and blood, a part of me I can't change. It can only have one name. I love her.

I fell before I even realised I should try to catch myself, and now I'm entirely hers. In love with my best friend's daughter.

I tell her with the brush of my lips on hers. With the thrust of my tongue. I hold her head, that silky blonde hair cascading over my fingers, and alternate tender licks with filthy plundering of her mouth that makes promises I know I cannot keep.

It's just a kiss. I stay at a respectable distance—for a kiss—so she doesn't find out how this is affecting me. I continue lying to myself that one kiss doesn't make me all the things I know I am.

But how can something wrong feel so incredibly right?

She's making whining noises and shifting on my legs. It's only when I sense her heat that my heartbeat skips. She has slipped to one side on my lap, so her pussy is flush to my thigh, separated by only a couple of layers of thin fabric. Her leggings. My trousers. And as I feel her move, I realise how, in the sinuous shifts that make her shudder with pleasure, she is trying to get contact on her clit.

That makes the room stuffed with air. Too much, and my head is swimming. She's... Turned on. Really, really turned on by our kiss. I enjoy her sensual movements, my hands slipping to her hips for a few seconds, taken aback at how sexy she is and how deliciously uninhibited.

Her sounds of frustration tug at my heart. Surely it wouldn't be a bad thing to give her what she needs? So long as I wasn't taking anything for myself, would that really be so wrong?

My lass needs to come.

"You think I don't know what you're doing?" I say, low and hoarse.

She gasps like a guilty schoolgirl, then whimpers and grinds harder. Part of me wants to take over. Flip her over and finger her, lick her, then make her come on my cock. But perhaps she needs this. To pleasure herself with a big beast and pretend she's a shameless hussy doing it without his knowledge. Maybe to stray into the forbidden before she settles down for a normal life somewhere else, far away from me.

I can't think about that.

All I know is I'm going to enable her to take whatever she needs from me, right now. That's my reason for existence. To be here for her.

"So naughty," I whisper and nip her earlobe. She speeds up. "You're getting off on this, aren't you?"

"No." Her hair caresses my chest through my shirt as she shakes her head.

"Liar," I insist. "And for that lie, there's a punishment." I grasp her buttocks in both hands and she squeaks as I pull her up and forwards. Her soft stretchy leggings are yanked down in a single tug and her white lace knickers follow. So fucking cute but I want her skin on mine. I have to feel her juices coating my leg as she writhes and moans.

Her eyes are wide as I hold her arse with one hand and unbutton my jeans with the other. There's a hint of trepidation around her open mouth as I push the fabric down and reveal my solid length covered with my boxers.

"Go on then, bonnie lass." I let her sink back onto my thigh, skin to skin this time. "You're so dirty, sweet, and beautiful." I cup one hand on her naked bottom and plunge the other into her hair. "You like the taboo, don't you? Make yourself come."

She moans as she begins to move again. I urge her faster. And fuck this is insane. My thigh is not sensitive. In thirty-eight years of life, no part of my thigh has ever struck me as being capable of more than a passing sensation. Not like my cock or my fingers. But it seems that every nerve ending in my body has migrated to where she's rubbing her hot soaking sex on my leg. Even the feel of her bare arse under my fingertips, pressing into her skin, isn't as good as her pussy.

"That's it," I tell her, whispering into her hair as she begins to shake with the effort. "My perfect lass. Give it up. Cream all over me."

I want to feel her come. My cock is harder than it's ever been from imagining it's not my thigh, but that solid length that she's using to pleasure herself. Or maybe it is just the sound of her. The wet, sticky noise of her pussy lips, the rustle of her top against my shirt. The falling snow outside insulates us from the usual hoots of owls or whistle of the wind. There's only the soft crackling of the fire and her breath, all high and desperate and ragged now.

She is way off-limits. I'm going to hell for this, if not all the other immoral and illegal things I've done. But my good lass deserves an orgasm. And while I'd love to feel her clench around my cock, she's my best friend's tipsy daughter. My dead best friend, lest I forget. Duncan would murder me for doing this.

Her making herself orgasm against my thigh isn't so bad, right? I'm not claiming anything I shouldn't. I'm not taking her cherry. I'm not pounding her into the sofa. I'm just... Here.

I'm practically an inanimate object.

Oh god I'd like to be her dildo. I'd be terrible. I'd never be able to keep still. I'd do everything for her pleasure, but

I'd take too. I'd find that spot which made us both pant and groan.

I am *not* an inanimate object as she uses me. I'm telling her she's hot and sweet and listening to her soft whimpers. I'm telling her how good she is and how amazing she feels. I'm tensing the muscles in my thigh so I'm harder for her, more solid to rub against to get her off more strongly. I'm smoothing my hands down her back and over the curve of her arse.

"Mo chridhe. My love," I whisper into her hair, but I swear she hears by osmosis because the next second she's juddering on my thigh. Then she cries out and shakes uncontrollably, head buried in my shoulder. That's a good thing, because if I watched her face as she came she'd see my terrifying possessiveness of all her beauty.

I hold her to me and make circles on her back, murmuring more words of praise and reassurance like she's completed a marathon rather than made herself come. But with the angle and the friction, I bet her legs are burning with the effort required to keep up that frantic pace.

As she stills, I gently press her forwards and she utterly collapses onto me, head nestled into my shoulder.

I don't say anything. My cock is so hard I could use it as a hammer. But the desire for her isn't what fills my brain, or even my whole body. A tendril of her soft hair tickles my nose and I leave it. She's the best thing I've ever held in my arms and there's a feeling in my chest, swelling and pushing on my ribs. Deep affection. The sort that rises from some dark part of your soul. A pinprick setting off a chain reaction and building into a star, a burning fire of heat that consumes all matter and radiates light.

Love. We have all this history together, her father had

my respect and friendship, and she's gorgeous and brave and smart. My grip on her tightens and I have to force myself not to squash her to me.

I have an inferno of love for my best friend's daughter. I want everything from her. Marriage and babies and to be at her side, helping her achieve anything she wants in this life.

And I cannot do anything about it.

Nothing.

When she puts her soft cheek onto mine, it's tentative. Questioning. I hold myself back from devouring her, instead meeting her lips with a kiss that conceals my savage desires, and gives, like before, only a contained part of myself as I replace our clothing. After her orgasm she's pliable and lets me care for her.

"Time for you to sleep." Because much as I'm dying to have her in my bed, my conscience is right. But my words sound tender and affectionate in a way I didn't intend, but do mean.

I'll remember this sweet, whisky-laced moment. I can already feel how my skin has absorbed it. My heart has tucked away the memory safe between the pulmonary artery and the right atrium.

"Yeah." She folds her arms and the look of hurt on her face almost breaks me. "Sorry about that."

Much as I want to reassure her, I don't.

It ought to be awkward as we walk upstairs together, but although she's not talking, I sense that she has realised why anything more would have been disastrous. I guide her to her room when she hesitates on the landing, and open her door for her.

I attempt a smile, but it doesn't reach my eyes. She does too, but it's as sad as mine.

"Goodnight, mo chridhe."

I don't wait to hear her reply. I head down the corridor to my own room. Alone.

5

MIA

It's still snowing in the morning and the tension in my chest eases. I have a little more time here. With my dad's best friend.

I lay in bed last night and thought about James and what he meant to me in the past, and what he means to me now. I thought about all the ways he was everything I wanted. Safe and strong and hot af.

Downstairs, James is in the kitchen, staring out at the snow. When he looks up he smiles and my heart goes wild. Is he too thankful that the storm hasn't abated?

He doesn't mention what happened last night, and neither do I. When I see his thighs encased in perfectly fitted denim though, as he comes out from behind the kitchen island to give me coffee and sit at a safe distance across the table, I actually salivate.

My wet pussy was pressed to him. Right to his skin. And I felt his erection, undeniable proof that he wanted me.

I'm so busy with his thighs, I don't ascertain if he's hard again this morning before he takes a seat.

Despite my protests that I don't need anything special,

he makes a full English breakfast, complete with black pudding, rolling his eyes when I protest.

It's... honestly not as bad as I expected? Like strong-tasting sausage, which with soft white bread feels perfect for this weather and the bleak Scottish landscape. Pretty tasty when I add lashings of his homemade tomato ketchup that has a spicy kick.

"What would you like to do?" he asks as he clears up our plates.

A multitude of replies tear through my mind and nearly come out of my mouth. *Lose my virginity to you. Be your lass forevermore. Get pregnant so I'll have a part of you with me even if you won't allow me to stay. Suck your cock.*

"Repeat what we did last night," is what emerges.

James slowly straightens from where he was placing our plates into the dishwasher. Gripping the thick mahogany brown work surface, he seems to be holding himself back.

I wait. And wait.

"I showed you the antiques in the snug," he replies eventually and my stomach, full of the food he made me as it is, plummets.

When he meets my gaze I know. For sure. It's full of so much heat I might spontaneously combust. I have no need for clothes, even in a snowstorm, when his green eyes are hotter than the sun.

He deliberately misunderstood what I said.

This is his way of keeping his distance, despite what he thinks I didn't hear last night as my orgasm overtook me.

My love.

This is going to be a fight to get him to accept that what is between us is not only inevitable, it's right.

"Sure." I nod innocently. "I'd love to see *everything*."

He pins me with a look that says, *Behave.*

Nope. No way.

I'm not letting him go.

Exploring the castle takes all morning. It's huge, yes, but I linger over each room. I ask him where he got every piece of furniture, and listen to each story of whether it came with the castle, he had an interior designer acquire it, bought it at an auction, or from an antiques dealer. I imagine going with him to those places and finding new things, because some of the rooms are a bit sparse. Lifeless.

I tell him he needs a cat and he agrees.

Pushing my luck, I suggest a dog too, and he nods again.

He has this whole life and I want to wrap myself up in it, pretending he's showing me and agreeing to my suggestion of pets to gain my approval, because I'm going to stay with him here. Always.

I try to tempt James. I honestly have no idea what I'm doing, so it's mainly drawing attention to my body and beds. By placing myself on said beds. Both of which he assiduously does not look at or touch.

His hand hovers at my back frequently, an inch from me but sometimes brushing my baggy jumper. His gaze never dips below my mouth.

But he has a hard-on. I can tell, because I have no such qualms; I don't look away from his body. I see him adjusting his jeans when he thinks I'm examining a painting, and on the way out of one of the bedrooms I swear he palms his cock.

The sight melts me like a dusting of snow dripping from a tree branch in bright sunlight.

When we get to the tenth bedroom I hear him groan as I exclaim eagerly and throw myself onto the bed. This is a four-poster, all rich velvet drapes and dark wood.

"So comfortable," I say, then take the direct approach. "Come and lie down here with me. Please?"

I think he's going to protest and stay away as he has every other time I've said he should try this bed, or see the view from where I am. Apparently, all I needed to do was tell him unequivocally, because although with visible reluctance, he not only comes within reach, he actually lies down on the coverlet opposite me.

I'm gleeful until I see his tortured expression.

Even then, I'm certain I can manage.

"Don't." He almost smiles but it's so sad, I'm stopped in my tracks.

"Please?"

"You don't have to. I'll help you and care for you without that, mo chridhe."

I open my mouth to say I wish I had *that* and everything else.

"I'm too dangerous and scarred for your beauty," he mutters. "Your dad would want you to be with someone your own age. Not a grumpy old bastard."

I screw up all my courage. "You're not grumpy with me."

This time his smile is genuine, if rueful. "I guess not, because you're you."

It's as good as him saying I'm special, and so even when he warns me, my heart sings.

"Don't push me, Mia. I'm not a saint. I've done a lot of bad things in my life. Don't let..." He breathes in and considers his words, "This be one of them. I never want you to have any regrets."

Me? Have regrets? He has no idea.

I watch his broad shoulders as he rolls away from me and stands. Everything he just said makes me twice as determined. I am not going to regret this, and I feel certain that with all his nurturing affection—that he isn't grumpy with *me*—the only regret either of us will ever have is if I leave here without him having been inside me and claimed me for his own.

For lunch, he cooks us creamy vegetable soup—gotta have my five-a-day he points out—with crusty sourdough bread slathered with salty butter.

I notice him watching my mouth again, and lick my lips more than strictly necessary.

"And what do you want to do this afternoon?" he asks indulgently.

"Do you have another castle for us to explore? With lots of bedrooms."

A grunt of what sounds like discomfort escapes him. "No more castles, sorry. But the thunder has passed. We can go outside."

"Really?" I think my eyes light up, because James laughs and tweaks my nose. Childish as the action is, it speaks of fondness and brings him close enough for a second that I can see the silver in his stubble.

It fills me with the longing to feel it, sandpaper on my skin. "I don't have anything to wear." My small bag didn't have room for bulky winter hats and coats.

Concern furrows his brow. "I'll get you all the clothes you want and more. Once the storm clears." That statement seems to pain him. "In the meantime, we'll make do."

He dresses me in his jacket—deliciously oversized—and rolls up the sleeves for me. After that he picks a tartan scarf, a pair of fleece-lined gloves that make me look like a clown but are warm and fluffy on the inside, and a soft grey beanie hat that he pulls over my eyes. I grumble and drag it back up with clumsy fingers to find him looking down at me with a gooey expression that makes my tummy flutter with a summer's worth of butterflies.

Outside, the snow falls in lazy floating specs as James points out where we should be able to see the mountains he calls Munros. All there is in the distance is speckled white, a perfect textured video background from one of those lifestyle videos of women in elegant mohair sweaters. I can see only the outlines of his home, a pencil sketch as he shows me where the limits of the walled gardens are, a terrace, spindly naked trees and bushy dark evergreens pointing to the sky and trying to spear up out of the snow.

"You'll love this view in autumn. It's beautiful lit up with yellow and red leaves." He points to the stick trees on the edge of visibility before it's all white. "Here, look."

I move close to see from exactly the right angle, and as he lowers his arm, his hand brushes mine and I slot it into his. Without either of us acknowledging, our hands find each other's, and he squeezes my fingers through the multiple layers of gloves.

He shows me every building and vista, half proud, half embarrassed, I think. As well as the castle, there are a dozen stone barns and courtyards for storage and leisure. But the way he talks—describing how different places are in spring when the vivid lime green shoots come out and the bluebells, and the red roses in summer—I wonder if he's assuming I'll be here. It makes my heartbeat surge.

Everywhere we walk leaves a pattern of my smaller footprints and his big-footed strides and although I know that the snow is transitory, being covered even as we tromp through digging channels, it feels like a contract.

There's a large flat lawn that is ideal for making a snowman. It doesn't take much persuasion and he's helping me roll a massive body, then a head. Sticks for arms and bits of gravel to make a face, and we stand back to admire our work.

It's not done yet though. I slant a look at James. He has a green tartan scarf hanging loosely over his neck that would finish our snowman perfectly.

"See the problem is..." I snatch the scarf by one tasselled end and go to wrap it around the snowman.

"Oh no way." He lunges for the scarf. "That's mine. It's not going on a snowman."

"What?" I yank the scarf to me and stumble backwards. "It's the rule! Snowmen have to have a scarf!"

"Uh-uh." He stalks towards me. "Not my favourite scarf. Give it back, Mia."

"Nope!" And I don't know why, but I take off as fast as I can in the deep snow. "Mine now!" I toss the lure over my shoulder.

I know as soon as he's coming after me because he's not subtle or small. He crashes through the snow, a yeti, the abominable snowman.

I hold the scarf out, a trophy and bait, and propel myself forwards. I only make it a short distance, enough to force my heart to pump.

It's only the scarf he wants, of course, but being chased by James, being wanted, sends a thrill down my spine. Blood pulses through me. I feel alive and vivid in a way I haven't for years.

He grabs for the scarf and I tug it. But he's so much stronger than I am, all I succeed in doing is spinning around and wrong-footing myself, tripping into a deep snow drift on the edge of the area we have cleared for the snowman.

I let out an oof of surprise as I fall backwards into the snow.

"You okay?" James is over me immediately, scanning me with his face pinched with concern, scarf forgotten.

I blink up at him. Yes. Yes I'm very alright with him over me like this, all bulk and strength and tender solicitude.

"Uuuhhh." I play up the really very minor amount of pain. "It hurts."

For a second there's panic in his expression, then he sees through my act.

"Do I need to check for broken bones?" he asks dryly.

"You could kiss it better," I suggest, licking my lips.

"Kiss chase, then?" His gaze drops to my mouth and when he meets my eyes again, something intent and hungry gleams in them.

"Could be." I'm way more out of breath than our tussle justifies. It's James. He makes my lungs forget how to work because my whole body yearns for him.

"Do you like being chased?" he murmurs.

"Yes."

"What about being caught?"

"I like that too," I admit in a whisper.

It's snowing. By all rights I should be cold, but I'm not even slightly. I'm burning up.

"Well, we can play chase." His eyes are dark as he looks at me, vivid and dangerous, almost impossibly green against the white snow. I shiver with anticipation. "But if I catch you, it might not be such an innocent game."

Threaten me with a good time, why don't you? My heart leaps. "Oh yeah? What will you do if you get me?"

"I'll make you pay," he says roughly. "I'll take revenge for last night, when you left me aching and rock-solid and unsatisfied."

I open my mouth to point out that it was entirely his

choice to be all ridiculous moral compass about my dad, but the warning in his expression makes my jaw snap shut again.

"And for teasing me all morning. Those stretches you do to push out your tits, and swaying your arse. I saw you pressing your thighs together to get friction on your clit."

I can't speak now. He saw things I didn't even realise I was doing and he *wants* me.

"I was so hard last night, and I couldn't risk touching myself with you so close. I couldn't be sure I wouldn't shout your name or lose control and storm into your bedroom, find out what you were wearing in bed and rip it off, and finish jerking myself to a painful completion all over your soft sleepy warm skin."

My eyes must be round as snowballs. I have to see him masturbating over me. I wish he'd done it so I could have the memory of his come on my body. I could have dipped my finger into where he marked me and tasted him.

"So when I say revenge, wee bonnie lass, you should understand that what I mean isn't cute or romantic. It's savage. It's animalistic."

Oh god his voice is low and threatening and I'm not at all certain I can cope with whatever he might dish out.

I haven't done anything like this before. Does he know? It would make a difference if he did, I think. He's too kind, and that stupid honourable streak would come out again. But what if... The thought begins as a whisper. Then it gets louder and louder. It's a shout so loud I'm surprised James can't hear it.

He could be the one to take my virginity.

James.

Even as revenge for making him suffer with a hard-on all night, I know from the cooling tips of my toes to the stray snow-covered ends of my hair that my first time with James would be good. He's older and experienced and he'd make it hot and sexy and more memorable than anything in my drab life so far.

"So you'd better be certain before you rush off, wee lass. You can walk away, and we'll not talk anymore about it." He sounds matter-of-fact, but I can see a line of tension at the corner of his mouth that says it would cost him. "But if you run, I'll be coming after you for what I'm owed."

6

JAMES

If she wants to arouse all my base instincts, she's going about it the right way. The need to claim Mia thuds through my body. Claim, have, fuck, breed.

I stare down into her eyes, trusting, but also glittering with challenge. She's so much. My lass deserves everything good in life and if that includes a very grown-up game of chase? I'd rather she did that with me. In fact, the thought of her with another man makes jealous fury ignite my chest. No. Absolutely not.

It's a good thing I didn't know how beautiful she has become or I'd have kidnapped her, consequences be damned. She's mine.

I want her, and I don't want to hold back anymore. Unless she tells me to stop bloody soon, I'm going to pin her down and get my tongue on that sweet pussy and make her come. I can almost taste her arousal; my mouth is watering.

I cup her bottom and indulge in kneading it a bit. She's soft and the right amount of firm. Then, holding her to me, I rise to my feet in one smooth motion. Mia didn't expect that, and squeals, clinging to me.

Although she's just there, arms around my neck, chest flushed to mine and blue eyes taking me in, I don't kiss her. Instead, I allow her to slip gradually down my body until her feet touch the snow again. And I'm certain from her expression that despite the layers of fabric she felt my erection every inch of the way.

I don't let her go until I'm sure she won't wobble. Shifting backwards, putting space between us, I stare down into her eyes. She's a clear sky on a stormy day. But instead of reducing the tension, the gap increases it. Like elastic being pulled out tight, I can feel the tug that will bring us back together. Faster. Harder. Violent.

"What do I get if I manage to evade you?" She blinks up at me, all faux artlessness and saucy tilt to her chin.

"Anything you want," I reply.

She slants a sceptical eyebrow and my answering huff of laughter is wry. Her doubt is proof of how sweet and untouched she is. Any other woman would already have seen right into how much I adore her. How I'm building into being obsessed. I'd give Mia everything. My ill-gotten gains and my heart on a plate, if she'd be *mine*.

"Think about what you want, Mia. If you evade me, you can claim your heart's desire. But if I catch you..." If I grab her, I'll indulge my need, and damn principles, what her father and my best friend would have thought, or the opinions of the far-away world about a man twice her age being with an unsullied angel like her.

"If you catch me..." She smiles, cheeky and light.

"Go on then."

She's waiting, tension in every line of her body.

"Run."

She sprints, coat flapping, and I watch her shapely calves in those leggings. A grin spreads across my face as she casts a teasing glance over her shoulder as she sends white powder in arcs from her heels.

I don't wait. I take off after her, my longer legs eating up the distance. She makes for the barns that I showed her around earlier, full of cars, machinery and dozens of nooks to hide in.

Canny, so clever, my lass. Blood throbs in my veins and pulses in my cock. I was already erect, but the pursuit of the one who will be mine sends more blood there. I'm running for the savage delight of the burn in my legs and chest.

I've done this before, of course. Chased someone down. But not for three years, and never without a gun in my hand or with a hard-on solid enough to use as a baton. It's unique. This thrill of the hunt. I hadn't realised I had missed this aspect of being a mafia kingpin.

Some mafia bosses are more hands off, letting their underlings take all the risks. But being untouchable has its own gamble. By sending young men off to do your dirty work, you might create resentment, not loyalty. And that's what gets you a bullet in your forehead.

That or having a jealous brother you're too kind to dispose of.

I pause at the corner of a barn and listen intently. The snow muffles all the sound, but it also means she can't move without a crunch as her feet sink in.

Nothing.

"You can't hide. I'm going to catch you, Mia," I call out.

She giggles, and I dive to the right just in time to see her dash out of the other side of the barn. I run after her and get to the door as she rounds the corner towards the house.

Everything feels familiar but new with Mia, fresh after years of tinned food. With her it's all the good aspects of the past, with a delicious sheen of novelty.

The snow hampers both of us in running, making it hard going. I relish the burn in my quad muscles thrashing through the thick snow. I wonder if she's tiring, especially in all that cutely oversized clothing. That makes me push harder, to close the gap between us so she doesn't get exhausted.

I'm having fun chasing her. Hunting her.

I didn't know I needed to be silly and playful, or how I lacked it. To make snowmen and laugh over the dinner table with her. To exercise long unused skills in tracking and tracking someone down.

I had no idea how much I required her in my life, how intensely I missed her, but now she's here...

Increasingly, I'm certain I can't let her go.

She turns to check where I am and shrieks when she finds I'm behind her. "No!" But the look on her face and the laughter from her as she stumbles into deeper snow says, *Yes*.

My heart thuds as she slows and is within reach, the sound of her panting in my ears. I scan ahead for the best place to catch her.

A snow drift that I know has a yielding bank of heather bushes.

I grab Mia around the waist and tumble her into the soft landing, and she lets out an oof immediately followed by a delighted giggle that fades as I roll her underneath me.

Her blue eyes blink up at me, wide and trusting, a smile lighting her face and snow freckling her cheeks.

"You dare run from me?" I growl. "Now you're mine."

7

MIA

I squirm but his body weight, so heavy, holds me down.

"I've got you," he says, and it's half comfort, half claim. He's hardly even out of breath after our chase.

My chest is heaving but instead of feeling bad-panicky, it's good. Exciting and vital.

This is it. Not how I imagined losing my virginity, or giving my first blow job, or whatever James is going to do, but it's perfect. Perhaps he'll shove his big cock—he's a big man all over so I'm certain his cock will be a beast—down my throat. My clit pulses.

But where I expect him to reach for his belt, he doesn't. He covers me with his body, shielding me from the weather and the cold. With his hips, he pins me into the snow, pushing us both down until we're in our own personal mini-igloo.

"Mm. You're so good. Such a good bonnie lass." He strips off his gloves, tossing them to the side.

I must look surprised, because he smiles slyly. "Kiss chase, remember?"

I reach to bring him to me, to kiss his lips, but he firmly

takes my hands and holds them above my head. Then with a grip that's fierce but only just over the line into painful, he cups my chin.

Between his body on mine, my trapped wrists and his fingers digging into my face, I'm unable to move.

He covers my cheeks with the lightest kisses. Snow crystal kisses. It's gentle and tender, in stark contrast to how he's keeping me captive.

"You're so strong and brave, and you put up an admirable fight. But now you can relax and let me do everything. I'm going to take such good care of you, my sweet lass."

I'm entranced by his words in that Scottish accent, so rough and smooth all at once. The snow is still falling but the thick layer of white all around us gives the expanse of nothing a secure feel. Like we're on a post-apocalyptic planet, and it's only us in the whole world and now it's just a barren safe place with this magical castle filled with everything we need.

And him. James is all I need. I close my eyes and give in. I'm his. I'm caught and I like that he overpowered me.

"I have to taste you," he mutters against my throat. "Kiss you."

He rears up and strips off his jacket. I'm honestly opening my mouth to protest that one, he *was* kissing me, and two, has he noticed that it's still snowing, when he hushes me.

Like I'm his pet, he makes shushing noises as he slides his jacket underneath my hips—I lift them for him when he taps the side of my butt because I've apparently lost my own will now he's in control—and I accept his hushing me and don't ask the questions rolling around my mouth. *What are you doing, James? Maybe try not to get frostbite?*

Then he's tugging my leggings down with impatient hands, knickers and all, and I make a squeak of protest as a frigid snowflake touches my previously warm skin.

He ignores me, trapping my feet together and pushing them up. My knees fall apart, and I should definitely feel ashamed of being so undressed outside. But though my cheeks do heat, I don't care. He doesn't even bother looking for my permission before he falls onto my naked skin, covering nearly all of my now-exposed thighs and pelvis with his broad wool-clad shoulders.

The groan that escapes him as he clutches my outer pussy lips reverberates through me. Then he licks. All the way up my soaking slit. He laps me up. Exactly as he said, he tastes me. And OMG it feels amazing. The heat of his tongue, the cold of the snow, pleasure spiralling into me. The rumble as he makes an appreciative noise and the flick he does over my most sensitive part.

"Such a sweet, wet, welcoming pussy. You taste so good, lass," he murmurs onto my skin then he's burying his face in my folds and stroking with hard licks.

My hands grasp out to the sides as he lays siege to my clit, dragging out pleasure from me and amplifying it with his whole mouth. Soft lips and knowing tongue, the sharp rasp of his stubble heightens every sweet sensation until I'm arching and shaking. He grips my thighs and spreads me wider and as my pussy is even more open to him, it all feels more sensitive.

One of his hands releases me, and his blunt finger touches my entrance. Cold. Hard. Then slipping in, firm against my resistance. A cry of sheer need escapes me, so animalistic I can't believe it's from my mouth. But I'm beside myself. This is primal and undeniable. He's owning me out in the open, in the way only he can.

He's my tormentor and captor and all my hopes and comfort. His finger pushes in and out of me, causing a wail as he rubs the sensitive part of my inner wall. That soft place that makes every touch to my clit brighter and hotter. The combination of his wet but unrelenting tongue and his clever finger up to the knuckle is magic. It's snow in June coating a blown-open red rose, miraculously beautiful and impossible.

"Come for me," he orders. That might have been what set me off, but the second finger thrusting in and a hard suck on my clit is the last thing I know before I'm jerking and sobbing with the shock of pleasure that sweeps through my body.

In the corner recesses of my brain, eventually I begin to feel other things that aren't soft aftershocks of my pulsing clit and languidly replete limbs. The wool of his jumper is both cosy and rough on my inner thighs. My knees are covered in a light dusting of snow and so is James' hat. His fingers are still in me, easing in and out, firm and sure. The movement both prolongs the pleasure and is somehow soothing.

He kisses my hip and looks up. "I'll never forget that, lass."

It's only once he's pulled me to standing and brushed off the snow, and we've returned to the house, heading straight for the kitchen to warm up with a cup of tea, that I notice.

The snow is sparkling from the touch of a sunbeam.

No. I...

I move to where the floor-to-ceiling windows reveal the end of this time of just James and me, together. Thick snow still surrounds the house, but the thinning layer of cloud unveils unwelcome blue.

Treacherous bloody sun. I choose the blizzard. I need our private world where James whispers that I'm good, and doing well as he slides his fingers across my clit.

"We can leave now if you want." James' voice appears just behind me as his hand settles on my waist. "Or in the morning."

The sadness I hear in his words is echoed by my heart breaking.

"What if I wanted to stay?" I spin and look up into his face.

"You want to live here? With me?" He sounds utterly disbelieving.

"Yes." I reach out and touch him and he growls like a feral dog.

"Turn around."

I frown in confusion. "But..."

"I said, turn around," he repeats, low and menacing.

I huff. "Why?"

"Because I can't be sure I won't just take you up on your naive offer when you're looking at me that way. And there are some things you should know first."

8

JAMES

She looks askance at me. "No need to be a big grump." But she does as I tell her and her obedience shoots pleasure straight to my already hard cock.

"I am a big grump, that's the point."

"No, you're not." She shakes her head and the desire to fist that cascade of caramel waves moves my hand almost to her. I hover my fingers.

Without her blue eyes on me and her every emotion showing on her face I order my thoughts. My cock—well it doesn't soften, let's not ask for the impossible—but it doesn't get any harder.

"What would your dad have said?" The question is essentially rhetorical at this point. I'm going to tell Mia everything. I'll love this lass until the day I die. The only choice she has here is the distance I love her from. But fuck. My best friend. He'd have kicked my arse into the next decade.

"He'd want us to be happy," Mia replies with absolute confidence.

For a few seconds I doubt that. Then I really think back

to Duncan. Not the way I've built him up in my head, but the real person. He was harsh, but so is any mafia boss. He was fair too, loving to his daughter and kind when he could be without compromising anything else.

He was canny enough to give in to the inevitable and make it seem like his idea, too.

She's right.

If he had really thought Mia wanted to be with me, he'd have granted his blessing.

Probably told me I was a fucking dirty old bastard and given me a black eye. But I think he would've been pleased, in the end, that Mia chose someone who would put her above all else. Love her to the point of obsession.

"I'm going to give you two choices," I say, and her head tilts to the side. Listening. "If at any point, you want the first option, just take a step away. Because..." My fists clench so tight from the effort of giving her this choice. Of not just taking her. "The other might not be something you want to hear. And that's okay. I'll stop the moment you step forwards." Stop speaking. Stop hoping. *Never* stop wanting her. "Understand?"

I sound harsh even to my own ears.

She nods.

"Option one. I'll arrange for you to disappear, as I promised. You have a normal life. Anything you decide to do. You'll have money and a new identity and all the freedom you could wish for." The benefit of being a billionaire. I can provide for my lass. "If you're ever in trouble, you just come here and tell me, and I'll fix it for you. Whatever it is. I'll always be here for you."

Because I love her with every part of me. Even the hardened and scarred bits that never thought they were capable of feeling anything again. I adore her. Now she's come to me once and I've seen her like this, I couldn't fully let her go. I'd stalk her for the rest of my days, keeping her safe from a distance if she couldn't be with me.

She'd never know how I protected her though. I'd give her independence.

"Understand?"

"Yes," she says and there's no inflection. I can't tell what she's thinking, and that was the point wasn't it? So she had a choice without being seduced or pressured.

She's motionless. Too still.

But she hasn't taken a step away. She hasn't accepted the good, normal, sane option.

"Option two. You can stay with me, as you requested, and be mine. But Mia, know that I'm not going to be satisfied by a tepid, cautious thing. I won't let you go once you've come on my cock. I'll fill you up with my come and breed you. You'll have gorgeous, courageous kids we'll look after together."

She shifts slightly and my heart wrenches. I almost take that back, and say I'll compromise. Whatever she wants so long as she'll be with me to some extent. But that's not honest. I need everything, and I won't stop until I have her rounded with my bairn. She deserves the clear decision.

"I'll be insatiable, Mia. I'll want to come deep inside you every day and every night. I'll be a bossy son of a bitch, and you'll find yourself on your back, coming as I devour your pussy like a starving man, multiple times a day."

Her mew makes my fingers, crushed painfully into my palms, ache to reach out. Not knowing what it means is killing me.

"You can forget autonomy if you stay. I love you too much to stand by. I want to be everything in your life. I'll tell you how to do things and be demanding."

It's taking all my restraint not to shove her against the wall and take her right now. Claim her.

"If you prefer a normal life and a normal husband, you should walk away, Mia. I'm obsessed already, and it's been what? A day? I'm going to get worse."

It doesn't feel like a day. It feels like an epoch. Nothing will ever be the same after being with my lass. If she leaves, all the colour will bleed from my life. It'll be reverse snow, cold and dark that sucks up light and heat.

"It hasn't been one day," she whispers. "It's been a whole lifetime. We were always friends, weren't we?" she asks, a wee bit uncertain. "You'd have helped me. You cared about me."

"Yes." She's right of course. I always loved my wee pal. The funny daughter of my old friend. "But Mia, I didn't want you like this. It's... changed." Such an insubstantial word for how my love for her has grown and morphed by meeting her as an adult. "I'm not going to be able to only take you for dinner once a month. I'm not going to only be your friend. I need more.

"I need you as my wife, wearing my ring. I need you overflowing with my seed. I have to have your lips soft and swollen from my kisses and your hair on my pillow. And Mia, you should know." I take a deep breath. This could spoil everything, even if she's willing on every other deranged and filthy condition so far. I'm a beast and she should know the depths of my sordid desires. "I want your submission too."

She turns at that. Her face is open and wondering, a slight smile playing at her pretty pink lips. "James."

My name in her sweet tone of acceptance nearly undoes me, but I don't stop. I have to finish.

"I will have to have you tied down and taking my cock

in your mouth or your pussy. I would come on your breasts and your face. I would mark you as mine."

Her eyes go wide and my cock twitches. This discussion has to end soon. I can't control myself forever.

"And I'd be yours?"

How can she doubt it after I've said all that? "Mo chridhe, you'd be mine."

"And you're mine, James." She reaches out. "Yes. I'll have all of that. Every part."

I grab her up before she can change her mind, bringing her slight frame to me. And she climbs me like a tree, pulling herself up, gripping my shoulders until I take the hint and lift her by her plump bottom. Our mouths clash together in a kiss that's almost brutal. Teeth and saliva and lips.

I have just enough sanity to carry her to a bed, probably because she won't stop kissing me. On the second landing she grinds into me, the minx, and I very nearly put her down right there and fuck her for the first time on the stairs.

But I get her to my bedroom and toss her onto the bed. She lands giggling and already reaching for the hem of her sweater, pulling it over her head in one. I'm equally impatient. There will be days for taking off her clothes piece by piece, and delighting in every inch of her. There will be times for hauling only my cock from my trousers, flipping up her skirt and shoving her knickers aside.

But right now, we both understand what we need, stripping off our clothes in all haste. Skin to skin.

I fall on her, and she welcomes me into her arms, legs already parted to receive me. She's desperately touching the scars on my shoulders and back, kissing my neck and face as I align our bodies.

I didn't think I had any control left, but as my cock finds

the dip between her thighs, I manage not to instantly thrust home.

"I always loved you. Always. But now I have this firestorm of desire too. It's going to burn me alive if you don't let me in, mo chridhe."

"Yes. Forever yes."

I notch the head of my cock at her entrance. Where no man has ever been before. That shouldn't give me this primal delight, but it does. "I'm going to make this good for you."

"It will be." She nods and tries to drag me closer. Ineffectual, of course, because she's tiny and I'm much bigger than her, but gratifying. "It absolutely will be."

"I'll take it slow."

"Get that monster cock inside me like you promised."

I choke out a laugh as I push forwards, but she's not wrong. With our size difference we are invariably going to be a tight fit. The head of my cock presses into her softness, then meets resistance. Her virginity. I can't think about it too much or it'll be overwhelming. That she trusts me with her first time, that she's never done this before. I'll be the one to introduce her to every variation of sex in all its intimacy and pleasure. And I know her virginity will mean she grips me, but when I drive in until the bulge of the head of my cock is past that constriction, I pause both to let her get used to my invasion, but also because I might pass out. She's so wet and perfect. We were made for each other.

"Mia." I don't move further, even though my cock is demanding—yelling—for me to thrust deeper into her unimaginably good body.

"Yes. James." She combs her fingers into my hair and clutches my head to hers. I sink in another inch. I can't help it. The need to be fully inside her is too much.

"Does it hurt?" I'm afraid of the answer.

"Mmm." I feel her nod against my shoulder.

With a muttered curse I start to pull back.

She stops me, hooking both legs tightly around my thighs. "Nope. Nope mister, you're not getting away that easily."

"But..." Maybe I can manage just jerking off over her breasts and going down on her for the rest of our lives? That would be better than hurting her.

"Baby," she insists. "Fill me up with your come, remember? Breed me."

Oh... and now she says that as though they're things I've promised her, my brain lights up like the Blackpool Christmas illuminations.

I don't withdraw. I breathe, shift so I'm looking into her summer sky eyes, and push another inch deeper. Then another. She feels like heaven. Soaking and despite everything her body is accommodating me. The tightness is drawing me in further, greedy.

"And James," she gasps.

"Yes," I reply between gritted teeth.

"It'll be worth it." She strokes one finger down my knuckles, soothing *me*. "I know you wouldn't cause me any pain you didn't think was worth it."

"I'd save you all and any pain." I'd do anything for her.

"Yes, but it hurts so good. You're spreading me open. Making me yours."

That does it. *Making her mine*. With a groan, I push the last few inches, until I'm fully in her, pressed together and the head of my cock deep.

Oh god this is going to kill me.

"You feel too good, Mia. I have to move."

"Yes." She flexes her hips and I groan as I slowly pull

out almost all the way, until her pussy is clenching at the tip of my cock. Then I thrust back home. Easy this time. Right. So unutterably right.

I look into her eyes as I ease in and out, stroking her, adjusting to find the perfect angle. I touch her face with my fingertips and brush our noses together before kissing her. A soft, gentle, loving kiss in stark contrast to where I'm spearing into her. I've accelerated without conscious thought. Harder and deeper. I'm trembling with the intensity of our joining, like this is my first time too. It feels like it. The scent and taste of her as well as the indescribable pleasure is like nothing I've ever felt.

I've never been this open to any person, have never let anyone see me so vulnerable and unguarded. But Mia? With her, every filthy sexual fantasy is all wrapped up with love and tenderness. This isn't smoking hot sex *with* her. It's smoking hot sex *because* it's her.

"You're it, for me, Mia," I say against her lips, still unable to close my eyes because I have to see everything. I have to fill her up and claim her entirely. "And I'm going to breed you."

9

MIA

No one ever told me sex was this *close*.

Like, I knew there was a big deal about the pleasure, and people do all sorts of stupid things to have orgasms. Which, fine. I was aware of that and figured I wasn't missing out on much because I have fingers and an imagination.

But I was missing out. I didn't have this union with the man I love more than anything in the world, and the proof that he loves me too. The way James is holding and looking at me, there's no room for anything else. I can't doubt. This is forever love.

His body is on me protectively, and also inside me. There's nothing between us and I feel I could reach right into him, like he's lodged in me. And his weight. Oh god he's so big everywhere, and heavy, pinning me onto the bed. He traps me perfectly. It sounds ridiculous, but all his strength and power over and around and in me, and my brain can only see it as care. Safety. Love.

The feel of his skin on mine is incredible. I can't stop

touching him, caressing his shoulders and back as he ups the pace of his thrusts. Where I'm soft and podgy, he's firm and silky. The dark hair on his forearms and chest looks so masculine but feels like luxury. I pet him, smoothing my fingers over his hair, and he smirks. Amused at me, despite everything.

He's a big dangerous scarred beast, and he's *mine*.

And his cock. Oh yeah. His cock is rubbing the sensitive parts of my passage, tempting me into madness. Being underneath him is overwhelming.

That's just the physical stuff, and that would be enough. But his words too. In between long drugging, filthy kisses where he sucks my lip into his mouth, nibbles on my cheek and explores me with his tongue, he tells me that he loves me and that I'm his good lass. And I'm certain he'll say that as many times as I need, and I really, really do need. I crave his approval and getting it so easily? It's turning the tap of a deep, sweet water well in a desert. A sudden and miraculous excess of the very thing you have to have to survive.

James groans when I dig my nails into his muscled buttocks, urging him faster and harder. In response, or maybe retaliation, he hooks my knees and pushes my legs higher. That spreads me open further for him, and I gasp at how much deeper he goes on the next thrust.

"I wanted you from the moment you appeared at my door, Mia," he says, releasing my leg and tangling his fingers in my hair. "I needed to sink deep into your sweet wet pussy and feel you come on my cock."

I'd like to have enough brainpower to reply to his deliciously dirty talk in a sane way. But all I have is, "Your big cock feels amazing."

That's out of my mouth before I can think, and I'd

snatch it back if I could. But I can't come up with anything better, because I am destroyed by him.

And James doesn't seem to mind. He smiles and asks, "Yeah? It's all for you, Mia." Before he drives even deeper. He's pounding me into the bed, reckless and wild and sweaty. It's glorious.

"I'm going to love you and be inside you and make you come every single day from now on," he pants out. His green eyes have gone savage. "I'll never get enough of you."

"Yes," I whimper. I'm so near. I wasn't aware I could be this aroused without even a touch to my clit, but I can. I'm on the point of coming. It's so close, I'm...

"Do you want me to fill you up, mo chridhe?" he says in that low, rough voice, untangling his fingers from my hair and palming my hip. His hand presses between us. "You need to come and then I'll spill into you."

As though I needed his instruction, I break. I shatter into a thousand pieces as wave after wave of pleasure overcomes me. It's sharp and seamless and unrelenting, this feeling, and it tumbles over me from where we join. It reaches all the way to my toes and my fingertips.

"Mia!" James bites my neck, rams into me once, twice more, then shudders. His cock is seated in me, as close as two people could be, pulsing. He's spurting hot come into me, so much I'm full. I can feel that extra, more than his big cock. It's seeping at the edges, despite how snugly he fits.

I'm a boneless sated creature being covered and squished in the best way when he collapses onto his forearms, groaning. I'm entirely caught, unable to move. I'm so content.

There are a thousand words for what just happened. What James did to me. Taken. Fucked. Screwed. Bred. I probably don't even know most of them.

But I do know one thing: I've never felt more loved.

In the morning, I wake to James kissing down my tummy and pushing my thighs apart in a way that's so territorial and demanding, I'm flooded with need by the time his mouth touches my slit. I'm hardly even awake when I come on his tongue, clutching at the bedsheets, screaming his name.

Then I scrabble at his shoulders, incoherently begging him. And sweet, generous, clever man that he is, he knows what my morning brain is incapable of expressing in a sensible way, and thrusts into me. By the time he rolls us over, I'm finally awake enough to try being on top. And he encourages me, murmuring that I'm his good lass, and so hot and sexy riding his cock. He stares at my breasts, plays with my nipples, and slides his fingers through my hair. He can't not take over though, fucking up into me and finding my clit with his thumb. When I've come again—all over him as he puts it—he grips my waist and takes control, going harder and deeper until he comes inside me, the wetness so excessive it spills out onto his thighs.

Then he holds me tight in his arms and lifts me to the shower and I'm not saying we get distracted, but the water is cool before James shuts it off and wraps me in a forest green fluffy towel.

We've actually managed to put some clothes on when a phone rings.

James blinks. And I realise that it's a long while since I heard a phone ring and not just because I left my phone back at the Barnes' compound. Slowly he reaches for it. "Yes."

He listens, a scowl extending down his face, growing darker and darker. He strides to the window, and I follow. Outside, not only has the storm cleared, nearly all the protective snow that kept the world at bay has melted. Wispy clouds mix the white to the blue. In the distance, a rainbow is streaked across the sky. It must have rained all the snow away.

"I appreciate your information," James snaps.

Fear pools in my stomach.

"Thank you. That will do for now."

"What?" I demand as he hangs up.

"Your uncle is on his way. There's a tracker on your Land Rover."

"How do you know?"

James' gaze slides from mine and doubt, maybe even dread, shadows his green eyes like the sun has dimmed.

He must have had a spy in the Barnes mafia.

"You had someone watching out for me." I'm sure. It makes sense. His assurance that I was okay, knowing about my grades. And him. The James I knew before all of this.

He shoves his hands into his pockets then immediately changes his mind and draws them through his hair, agitated. His silence is eloquent.

And it's *so good*. All this time. I believed I was alone. I assumed no one bothered at all with what I did or thought, so I kept it all to myself. I thought James didn't care. But he tried to check up, and was probably only stymied by how effectively I hid my misery.

Visibly steeling himself, he looks into my eyes. "I'm sorry. I shouldn't have, but I had to know, Mia. Forgive me." It's a command, but under the hard words there's a tide of uncertainty and guilt.

"Nothing to forgive." I reach out and run my fingertips

along his jaw. Sandpaper rough, strong. *Mine*. How could he think he needs forgiveness for caring for me? Loving me when no one did. "I'm glad."

"I should have come for you immediately."

I shrug. "I'm pleased it worked out this way. If you'd seen the snotty years where I cried a lot, maybe you'd never have found me attractive."

James winces. "Let's not speculate on how you'd have tortured me with your sweetness..."

"You said you wouldn't talk to my uncle. Why?"

His lips tighten. "We don't have much time for me to explain, given we have to figure out where that tracker is. He's flying to Edinburgh now and will be driving the rest of the way. But suffice to say that he hasn't run the Barnes mafia in the manner your father did. I thought when Duncan died it was just the consequence of how we both liked to run our operations—leading from the front. But later, Barnes did things that Duncan drew the line at. Trafficking children... And I'm not so sure Logan didn't..." James tails off and the pain in his eyes cracks my heart right open.

He suspects my uncle murdered my dad. He thinks my uncle traffics children to... Yeah. I don't need to fill the gap. Stealing them is bad enough.

A thought pops into my mind. "My uncle tracked me with the car, right? He doesn't know this is your house. It could be a bed and breakfast for all he knows."

James shakes his head warily. "I presume so."

"I've got an idea."

I park my Land Rover in a quiet spot a few miles outside of a village an hour away from James' castle. His SUV is big and sleek and black and I feel small and ridiculous until James pulls me into his lap. Tucked up with my old Land Rover just in sight, we wait.

While we'd run around making preparations, and driving here, I didn't have time to think. But in the watery light of the cloudy day filtering in through the windows, sat with my head on James' shoulder, I allow myself to consider.

Is this really the best thing to do? It's not a question of where I want to be, that is by James' side. The more thorny issue is my Land Rover. Everything I own is in that vehicle and I'm wearing his clothes rolled up, and with a makeshift belt, just in case we're wrong about where the tracker is.

"What I don't understand is why he wants me to marry anyone?" I say into James' throat, then breathe him in and sigh. "Uncle Logan totally ignored me. He told me, on the few occasions our paths crossed, that I was a financial drain and a pest." A burden. But James doesn't seem to mind my weight, either on his thighs or in his life.

James shrugs and his gaze flickers briefly from the Land Rover, to me, then to the tablet on the dashboard that shows the movements of cars in the vicinity. He tightens his hold on my waist. "Same old motivation."

"I guess he really wants whatever pitiful amount of power would come from selling me as Duncan's daughter."

He barks out a laugh. "Not that."

Admittedly it did sound unlikely to me too. "What then?"

"Did you not know that you're wealthy? Duncan left you enough money and more."

I gape.

"Hmm. We'll sort that out as soon as we're finished here and I've bought you some new clothes."

"You're kidding me." I had wealth all this time? I could have... Maybe not done that much before I was eighteen, and that realisation causes things to slip into place. It was my birthday only last month. No one makes a fuss about the day anymore, so it came and went without any fanfare, so I assumed I was just going to continue to, as my uncle put it, sponge off the family business. If I'd thought I had my own funds, I would have done things very differently.

James leans in and rubs his nose to mine. "Why would I lie to you about this? I have plenty of money for both of us. The only reason you should claim it is because it's yours, and Duncan would have wanted you to have it."

"My dad did plan for my future," I whisper. I had no idea.

James goes stiff.

I turn and there, by my Land Rover, is a figure in a smart dark coat. With him are two goons in similarly bleak attire. I shiver.

Call it instinct, or intuition, but I'm sure James is right about everything. Attempting to sell me off like a chunk of steak is the least of Uncle Logan's crimes. I pick up the remote from the passenger seat.

"Mo chridhe," James says, voice low. "You don't have to do this. I'll quietly dispose of him if you prefer."

"What does it mean? Mo chridhe."

He cups my cheek and looks into my eyes. His irises look like the promise of spring and new life. Green in the depths of winter. I lean into his warmth.

"It means *my heart*," he says with soft urgency. And it's my heart that expands like a balloon. Yes. He's my heart, and I'm his. "I love you."

"Good, because this is the real commitment." He shoots me a wry smile.

"It's true, I'm more-or-less sacrificing my dog here." I glance over to where one of the goons has unlocked the Land Rover and my uncle is rooting through my rucksack. They're all right beside it. The ideal moment. Presumably not finding what he's looking for, he looks up and I swear that even over the distance our eyes meet.

"This is for the kids," I whisper, and press the button.

The fireball is twice the size of the vehicle and probably I ought to be shocked or faint in some girly way. But I don't. There's just the satisfaction of having done the right thing.

James presses a kiss to my temple. "I'm proud of you."

"It was your skills that made it happen," I reply, and slip into the passenger seat. My deadly lover. "Now, you promised me clothes, breakfast, marriage, pet animals, and babies, in that order, Mr McQuoid. You see what I'm capable of if crossed."

"Sexy, demanding, and dangerous," James laughs as he starts the engine. "Mia, you're perfect."

EPILOGUE
JAMES

5 years later

"I bought you a new coat. You don't need to wear that one that doesn't fit anymore." I put on my sternest glare as I enter the porch.

She turns and looks at me, unafraid, pouting, a tendril of her dark hair over one green eye. "I like this one."

For crying out loud. "But I just bought you a new one, so you should wear it. We went shopping together for it only last week. And *that one doesn't fit.*"

"I told you Daddy would be upset you didn't want to wear your new coat."

My eyes meet Mia's over our elder daughter's head. Our youngest is more pliant to what she wears, since she's still nursing, strapped to Mia's chest and asleep in a pink hat and mittens.

"Don't care." Iona storms out of the house in her wee boots and coat that shows a full inch of sweater beneath the cuffs. It's way too small.

"Are you going to try and get her back?" I ask Mia.

She shrugs and shakes her head. "Thanks for the offer, but I think I'll opt for you warming her up when she gets cold."

I nod. Mia's right. "I'll commission a custom-made version of that coat until she's bored of it."

My wife laughs. "She'll be going on dates aged eighteen in a coat with pink snowmen."

"She will not be going on dates aged eighteen." No way. Not my wee daughter.

Mia laughs even harder, and I grumble, dragging on my boots before I wrap my arm around her waist as we head out into the crisp cold day. The sun is white in the blue sky, and Iona is making another snowman on the main lawn.

On the hill the Highland cattle Mia insisted on having paw the snow to get at the grass, braving the weather. The dogs and the cat are somewhere nearby, causing mischief no doubt. The goats and sheep are undercover, as is Mia's precious Land Rover. It took me months to find an exact match to the one she had to sacrifice, and she keeps it tucked warm in the garages. She doesn't drive it much, because the lassies are too young to travel in it, but I know sometimes when I'm looking after our bairns in the summer she takes a book and goes and sits in it to read and feel close to Duncan. A place all her own to be with her thoughts. In addition to the whole floor of the main castle she's taken over and the estate covered with her animals.

There's so much to be grateful for. Mia. Our family. The wild and beautiful home we live in. When we had breakfast together after disposing of her uncle all those years ago, we talked about Mia taking over his position in the Barnes mafia. With my support as her henchman, of course. But in the end, she wanted to settle in my castle with our babies and lots of animals. More fun.

I'd already disappeared, and Mia's cousin, running Barnes, turned out to have no interest in hunting her down once he knew whose protection she was under.

So that was it.

"What is it with you lasses and clothes that don't fit?" I grumble, looking at Iona.

Mia nudges me with her elbow. "At least the clothes I like that don't fit are too *big*."

"Mmm. That is compensation." She knows I love it when she wears my shirts. "All the better for me to access..." I whisper into her ear, and she giggles. "If you weren't wearing so many well-fitting clothes right now, I could—"

"Not in front of the baby!" she laughs, light in her eyes. We both know how that bairn was conceived, after all. When babies are asleep, parents can play *all sorts* of sexy games.

I grin and lean over to kiss our second daughter's head, then brush a stray tendril of Mia's honey-blonde hair from her cheek. "Later then."

Mia nods eagerly.

"Daddy, Daddy!" Iona rushes over, green frog boots kicking up snow. "I need your help with the snowball for the snowman! It's too big for me to push!"

I widen my eyes. "Too much for even you, my wee lass?"

"Aye!" She has the sweetest accent that pivots between my Scottish tongue and Mia's southern plum-in-the-mouth.

"Then we'll *all* have to help." I take Mia's hand and we go to help make yet another snowman.

With luck, it won't be the only life Mia and I create today.

Thanks for reading *Forbidden Appeal*. For more steamy and forbidden age gap romances, read the rest of the Dad's Best Friend series in Kindle Unlimited.

Want to see what happens that evening? Get the exclusive extended epilogue straight to your inbox.

For another obsessed and possessive age gap mafia boss romance, Captured by the Mafia Boss is available in KU now.

EXTENDED EPILOGUE: JAMES

That evening

I place the baby monitors onto the sideboard and check the volume. Both my wee lassies are fast asleep. It's been twelve months since our youngest was born, and I know it makes me a bad man, but I'm itching to see Mia rounded with child again. All in good time.

Time to focus on my good lass. She's had a long day, and needs to let off some steam. Stop being a mum for a bit and just be her. My beautiful, desirable wife with needs of her own.

She's fussing in the kitchen, her shining hair falling out of its braid and curling at the spot next to her eye. I want to push that strand behind her ear and kiss the exposed skin.

"Mia." She looks right up at my tone. Hard. Cold. Uncompromising. "Come here."

Brushing the strand of hair from her eye—infuriating—she shakes her head. "I just need to—"

"That wasn't a request, mo chridhe. It was an order."

Her mouth twists but she chucks down the tea towel

and approaches.

As soon as she's close enough, I pull her roughly to me, scoop her caramel hair from her neck and wrap it around my knuckles. I breathe her in. Fuck, so sweet. I adore her.

"Who do you belong to, Mia?" I say the words into her neck.

"You," she moans as I kiss my way up to her mouth, dragging my lips over her soft skin and tasting the salt and musk. Delicious. She's so tasty I want to eat her up. And we'll get to that.

I turn her in my arms so her back is to my front, then give a gentle push. She bends obediently over the table.

"Are you wet like a good lass?" I ask, even though I know the answer. She always is.

"I'm not sure," she replies teasingly. "How about you check for me?" She wiggles her bottom.

Leaning down and starting at her bare heel, I run my fingertips up her right leg, slowly, savouring this moment of slow anticipation before I take her rough and hard. She writhes a little.

"So impatient," I scold tenderly, as though I'm not.

Ha.

I'm desperate to be inside her. I'm going to fuck her thoroughly.

When my hand reaches the hem of her fitted woollen dress, I hook it, bringing it up, as though that was my only intention. These gentle touches drive her wild. She gets more and more feral every time I take it slow and sensual, until in a week from now she'll pounce on me while I'm sitting at my desk or we're watching TV on the sofa, rip open my flies, and sit onto my cock, bouncing until she makes herself come.

Perfect. She is so perfect in every way, even when she's

hurried and horny.

For now though, she's at my command. And I'm loving dragging her dress up her body. Her golden skin that is revealed makes me even harder, and oh yes. Her white lace knickers cupping that beautiful peachy arse. I lose it a bit. Stepping closer, I shove my aching but still covered length against the cheeks of her arse. She moans as I grind against her, showing her how much I want her.

"Open up," I demand, kicking at her ankle, and she obeys instantly, shifting her feet outwards and revealing where I need to take her.

And she needs me. Drawing back, I shove those pretty white knickers down, exposing her pink folds. Wet. Soaking wet to the point that a line reaches down her leg to the fabric that had been covering her.

Seeing how much she wants this cracks my resolve. I grab her dress, and she helps me pull it from her body. And thank god. No bra. Her back is smooth and just slightly freckled from sunbathing naked in the sunshine earlier in the year.

"Want me to put another bairn in you?"

She rolls her hips and pushes her bottom up in answer, further exposing those pretty pink folds. "James. Now."

"Still no moving," I tell her, even as I groan and tug off my T-shirt. I need to feel her skin on mine, and I have to be inside her. I can't wait. I'm going to make her come over and over before I pump her full. Nothing better than watching my come leak down my wife's leg or drip from the tight seal of where we join.

I strip off my jeans and boxers in one, then I'm naked and so is she except for the lewd detail of her knickers around her thighs. I take my cock in my hand and give it a few rough strokes just looking at her, waiting for me.

"You're so sexy like this," I growl. "I love despoiling you as an innocent, but it's just as hot when you look like a good whore waiting for what she's going to be paid to enjoy."

She turns her head and no less than smirks over her shoulder at me. Oh yeah. She likes that game too.

"Remember when you wanted to have an indoor pool?"

She writhes and I can see she's trying to get friction on her clit. She remembers. I couldn't understand it at the time, her sudden insistence on serving me sexually when she knows I love to get her on her back and coming on my tongue, or coming before I do. I stroke myself a couple more times remembering when my wife decided she'd make up for the obscene amount of my money she wanted to spend by being my voluntary whore. Ridiculous really, since she could have paid for it herself easily. After a week of surprise blow jobs at my desk I forced her to confess. That also led her to be bent over a hard surface and thoroughly fucked. My desk in that case.

I take my cock and drag the tip through her honey-coated pussy.

"Please, please, James," she whispers, clutching at the table. "I need you inside me."

"I can't deny you anything." Least of all when it's what I need too.

Grasping her hips in both hands, I enter her in one brutal thrust, all the way to the hilt because she is so wet and ready.

She cries out as I split her open. It's always a tight fit, and fuck she's the best thing that's ever happened to me.

"Good lass."

I don't ease her into it, that's not required for us anymore. I begin to pound into her at the same time as she pushes back to try to get more.

"So greedy," I whisper. But she knows my favourite thing is her enthusiasm for pleasure. And for me.

The tight wetness of her is incredible. Overwhelming.

She sheaths me so tightly from this angle, and probably it's perverted, but the sight of her arse, the curve of her back and the profile of her face pinched with rising pleasure makes me impossibly hard.

My wife.

And the naughty daughter of my best friend. Years on, the taboo has faded and I'm left with twisted glee at how young and beautiful she is. That I was the first and only man to claim her and take her virginity. Those things add a sharp delight to the unrelenting tide of love that this amazing woman chooses to be mine. To submit to me.

All that is to say, I can't hold out for long. The feel of her clamped around my cock, hot and soaking, and the whimpered sounds from her mouth.

"Touch yourself." I like it when she takes the pleasure she deserves. "Make yourself come on my cock. Good lass."

I praise her as she moves immediately. One hand slips down to between her legs and I feel the difference as she starts to rub her clit. The way she pulses on my cock. And her other hand goes to her breast, tantalisingly out of sight. I know what she's doing though.

"Pinch your nipple," I command, not because she won't without my approval or anything like that, but because it's another connection between us. It's hotter when I order her to make herself come. And today it's all I can do to thrust into her and not come within seconds from the sheer pleasure of her welcoming pussy.

My fingers dig into her flesh as we slap together, my balls swinging even as they tug upwards, readying to fill her.

She tenses and her pussy tries to milk the seed out of me

as she comes.

"Don't stop, Mia."

A dissenting whimper escapes her lips. It's sensitive after having come so quickly and explosively. But she comes twice, that's the rule. And I can't hang on, so she has to push through.

I feel her circle her clit again. "Very good."

I keep up a forceful pace, dragging the underside of my cock on her inner wall where it feels best for both of us. "Yes, go on."

And thank god this orgasm springs up on her even more easily. Within a minute of my thrusts going ragged as I begin to lose control and think I'm going to come before she does, she's wailing like a banshee.

I only just have the presence of mind to put my hand over her mouth and muffle her cries of pleasure, leaning over her, my chest to her smooth back. Then I give in. One thrust, deep. Then another and I feel my seed rising. On the third I break.

I collapse onto her, letting her feel my weight pressing her into the table as well and spearing her.

The orgasm doesn't let up for a long time, rolling over me as I spurt into my wife again and again. Filling her up, just as I promised.

She turns her head, seeking me out, and I release her mouth. It takes a bit of twisting, but I get our lips to meet in a sweet press of lips. Fuck, this woman. She's everything to me, and I tell her with my kiss and the lazy easing of my cock into her pussy, mixing her wetness with my seed.

"You're mine, Mia." And I'm hers. Her dominant and her husband and—as she well knows—the man who would do anything for her.

"Yours." I feel her nod. "I'm always yours."

THANKS

Thank you for reading, I hope you enjoyed it.

Want to read a little more Happily Ever After? Click to get exclusive epilogues and free stories! or head to EvieRoseAuthor.com

If you have a moment, I'd really appreciate a review wherever you like to talk about books. Reviews, however brief, help readers find stories they'll love.

Love to get the news first? Follow me on your favored social media platform - I love to chat to readers and you get all the latest.

If the newsletter is too much like commitment, I recommend following me on BookBub, where you'll just get new release notifications and deals.

- amazon.com/author/evierose
- bookbub.com/authors/evie-rose
- instagram.com/evieroseauthor
- tiktok.com/@EvieRoseAuthor